Victory and Other Stories
Femdom Mind Control
Flash Fiction – Vol. 23

S.B.

Table of Contents

- A Saturday Like Any Other - 7
- Acceptance - 12
- Breaking Up - 14
- Courage - 17
- Digital Addiction - 19
- Discovery - 22
- Her Reputation - 26
- Living Madness - 29
- Moment - 34
- Past and Present - 37
- So Lucky - 39
- Victory - 42

They always win against your mind.

A special thank you to all patrons of Spell... B-O-U-N-D.

A Saturday Like Any Other

It was a Saturday like any other, nothing out of the ordinary happened.

Henry got out of bed at exactly 8:30 in the morning, took a warm, relaxing shower, shaved, and then proceeded downstairs for a hearty breakfast, dressed in nothing but his underwear. As he sat by the kitchen counter, warm toast in hand, he glanced at his phone, the guardian of his routine.

While he considered himself an extremely well-organized person, he wasn't much for remembering things on his own. His short-term memory was just atrocious, so he left it all at the hands of technology. The daily planner reminded him of everything that was important, and nothing was ever added to it that didn't qualify.

It was his day off from work, so there were fewer entries than usual waiting to be read. The first was a note about the last game in the basketball play-offs. The second simply said: Call Lisa.

"Who the hell is Lisa?" He muttered to himself. He was sure he knew no one by that name, but his phone had never led him astray before. He scrolled through the contact list and there she was, her name written in capital letters and with a winking emoji next to it. While he did not know what to expect, he did as his planner told him to.

The phone beeped twice, and then there was nothing but static. It crackled in his ears as if it were coming from an alternate dimension far, far away. Henry's eyes drooped as the familiar numbing sound enveloped him completely, telling him to relax and go to sleep again.

* * *

Lisa laid down the phone and looked down. Why wasn't she dressed yet? It was almost 9:15. Mistress Angel would be there at any moment and she had to look good. She left the kitchen in a hurry and disappeared inside her walking closet, looking for the perfect combo to greet her.

She found it in a long-sleeved black faux leather bodycon dress. It stressed her curves perfectly. Mistress Angel loved that, and she loved her so much. She freshened her make-up and her heart leaped with joy when the doorbell rang.

Mistress Angel was a mid-forties bleached blonde, petite woman - only five feet three in heels compared to Lisa's six-two - but she always made her feel small. The moment she opened the door, her piercing blue-green eyes overwhelmed her completely, forcing her to drop to her knees and kiss her thigh-high boots.

"Good morning, slave." Her owner said. Usually, she dispensed such greetings and got right down to business, but she was in a good mood that day and that was always a good thing.

"Good morning, Mistress." Lisa gulped as her tongue worshiped every inch of her soles, tears of happiness rolling down her eyes. "I'm so glad you're here."

"As you should be. Stand up and follow me. We need to go through your assignments for today."

"Yes, Mistress."

Lisa trailed behind her like a loving puppy desperate for more attention, Mistress Angel's presence dominating her from top to bottom. It was a feeling she treasured above everything else, rendering her completely helpless. In a distant past, she had tried to resist it, but the pain of doing so had been unbearable. Now, she just obeyed her supreme will, happy to have no thoughts of her own.

Mistress sat on her sofa and handed her a couple of pictures. They were all of the same man, a greasy Texan oil tycoon, and his equally abhorrent friends, people without scruples but with fat cocks that needed to be satisfied no matter what.

"You are to please all of them during the yacht ride this afternoon, got it? They'll pay extra if you swallow so be sure to savor every drop. I want my money."

"Yes, Mistress. It will be my pleasure to give it to you."

"You're a good girl, Lisa. I'm sure you'll make me proud. And when you get back home, you already know what to do."

"Yes, Mistress. Anything you say."

"That's a nice dress you're wearing, but I'm sure our guests will be happy with something trashier... lead me to your wardrobe and let's get this fixed right away."

Lisa complied immediately, mouth watering at the prospect of the wonderful meal she was to have in the afternoon.

* * *

It was almost midnight when she returned home, red lips smeared with salty cum. She was stuffed and tired, every orifice in her body drilled into exhaustion. It had been worth it though, just to see Mistress' bank account growing. She would do anything and everything for that pleasure alone.

Lisa took off her clothes, tossed them in the laundry basket, took a long shower and slipped into bed. Her phone laid waiting for her, a single note flashing on the screen: Call Henry.

She did not know who he was, but Mistress Angel did. She was her world. She obeyed Mistress Angel. The phone beeped twice before a world of blissful static wiped her mind clean.

* * *

Henry blinked and went to sleep. It had been a Saturday like any other, nothing out of the ordinary happened.

Acceptance

Hello. You must be subject number 21308. First, let me just say that, in over a decade breaking and training servants, I've never encountered someone with such resilience. I truly admire you resisted all conditioning so far, but enough is enough. You're so exhausted right now that controlling your thoughts should be a breeze.

Now, listen carefully. Focus on my words and my words alone, for they hold the key that can make your life whole again. Ever since the advent of humanity, you males thought the world was yours to dominate, and that women were inferior creatures that needed to be tamed when, in fact, it was the other way around. We were always better than you, stronger than you, the rightful rulers of everything that was and will ever be that you tried so hard to dispose of, using nothing but twisted logic and brute force. Luckily, we had other means at our disposal to bring about the true order, namely the innate ability to subdue a mind through hypnosis, the way I'm doing to you right now.

As you listen to my words, you're accepting them as the only truth possible... You may have been to withstand a great number of inductions before but not this one, not this time. Your mind is weak, your thoughts drained. The more you listen to my voice, the more you feel yourself falling into an abyss, plunging helplessly into the dark depths that consume all light and all will to resist. Within it, all false doctrines you were taught at birth fade away, replaced by this simple message: you are just a slave and nothing else, you must submit... you are just a slave and nothing else, you must submit... Repeat this mantra in your subconscious until it fills you completely... you are just a slave and nothing else, you must submit... you are just a slave and nothing else, you must submit...

Wonderful. By the way you're looking at me now, it's obvious you're coming to terms with your natural condition. Slavery always had your name on it, and now you can claim it. From now on, you will obey my every command and the orders given to you by all the women working under me. It's the least you can do after all the hard work you've given us. We will have a lot of fun with you until the next slave auction and then you'll be out and about, pleasing your new owner until she's had enough. Those are the rules since times immemorial, and I'll not be the one to change them. Now, come to me on your knees like a good, hypnotized bitch.

Breaking Up

Angie laid down the fashion magazine on the crystal table and finished sipping her cup of coffee before bothering to look up. William stood in front of her, wearing his Sunday best - i.e., absolutely nothing! - abs and delts on display. He had always been ripped but, with her rigorous training, he had taken it one step further. Silently, she admired his toned muscles without losing her composure. Royalty such as herself only showed lust when it was necessary, and that was not the time lest he started thinking he was anything other than what she had created: an obedient servant.

"You wanted to talk to me?" She crossed her legs and fiddled with her long, black hair. She was wearing her outfit of choice: a horizontal striped tank top and black mini skirt. Outdoors, she never went commando, but in the sanctity of her place, there was nothing better to tantalize him into further submission. A whiff of her scented pussy reached his nostrils, concentration waning. Pussy had never failed her before, and there was no reason to believe it would do so now.

"Y-yes." He struggled to have the words come out exactly the way he wanted them. "As much as I've enjoyed where our relationship has taken us, I think it's probably for the best if we just..."

"Time out." Angie flashed the old basketball sign and adjusted her body position on the wicker chair. A tuft of nicely trimmed pubic hair assaulted his senses. "You were saying?"

"Well... hm... you know I love you, but I think we should..."

"Break up?" Angie's right hand slid under the skirt, looking for Heaven. She found it right away.

"Can you please not do that?" He grumbled, his circumcised cock shooting up in the air like a flagpole.

"Is it bothering you?" Her crooked smile said it all.

"You know it is."

"Yet another reason for me to continue then, but let me see if I get this straight: you really want this to be over, huh?"

"Yes, please. It was fun for a while but now..."

"Now what?"

"I feel like we're not going anywhere and... there's someone else, sorry."

"Who?" Her eyes turned red. "Who's the bimbo?"

"She's no bimbo, but I'd rather not to tell you her name... for her sake."

"Afraid I'll give her the same pussy treatment I gave you, big boy?"

"Actually, yes." He crossed his arms. "It wouldn't be the first time."

"You're right." She pushed a finger against her labia and spun it in place, creating a mesmeric vortex of flesh that always made him feel weak.

"Please release me, Angie. You don't even like me! And wouldn't it be fun to train another slave, huh?"

"Fun? Probably." She mused. "But you make the best coffee this side of the Pacific. You really want me to miss that?"

"I just want my freedom back, please."

"Okay." She shrugged. "If that's what you really want..."

"Seriously?"

"Yeah. From now on, consider yourself free... to forget this conversation ever took slave and that you are nothing more than my puppet." She winked and so did her twat, a pink haze covering the space between them.

"Not again!" William sobbed as the magic mist clouded his memories until only feelings of mindless love and adoration remained. Perhaps one day, she would change her mind, giving him the solace he so desperately wanted, but it was unlikely. Succubi are possessive, and she loved his brews more than anything. For those alone, it was worth keeping him as a slave.

"Get some more done." She commanded as she turned on the TV. Her favorite reality show was about to start.

Courage

Hi and thank you for stopping by. You know, I can feel your emotions even from a distance. I have that gift. It's not exactly empathy but something similar, and I'm picking up all these strange vibrations right now... desires of both body and mind that you've been hiding all your life, a need of deliverance from the social role you've been asked to play since an early age even though no one bothered to ask you if you wanted it.

I can visualize how your spirit conformed to those expectations, creating a picture of order that became you. Everything inside your intellect is in a unique place, perfectly categorized... rules and principles of existence written in large volumes and placed in heavy bookshelves stretch out almost indefinitely, giving you the impression that you have no other choice, that you must fill the shoes you've been given under penalty of being deemed useless and insignificant...

... but that's not true! Not true at all. You can fight those impositions and live out your fantasies. You can reach for the inner strength to knock down those shelves... and that's where I come in. I can share with you the power required to finally break free from the shadows of the past, and I'll do just that if you'll be so kind to continue listening to me and imagine you're staring into my eyes. Raise your chin up in your mind's eye so that your gaze meets mine and then look deeply into it. Notice the self-assurance that lights my soul from inside out. I'm passing it onto you right now... take it!

Yes... feel this essence touching your lips like the sweetest of kisses and making you whole. See yourself next to the archive of your imagination and pushing it at one end, creating a domino effect that will obliterate all the falsehood of yonder days... all that will remain is that yearning desire of not having to think any more, of being eternally submissive and accepting that such a life isn't a sign of weakness, but of utmost determination. It takes more courage to serve than to be in control all the time and, at the hands of an understanding dominant woman such as myself, you'll experience a bliss beyond comparison.

Listen... let go... surrender... yes, just like that... you're doing great, sweetie. Courage will never fail you again.

Digital Addiction

Theresa Raines rotated the front door's handle and peeked inside her daughter's house.

"Allison? Are you there?"

Silence. She was almost certain that would be the case but had to make sure. Not much for entering other people's houses uninvited - and with a duplicate key to boot! - she would feel even worse if she had to lie to her face and say the door wasn't locked or something. The sexagenarian sneaked inside and welcomed the darkness of the main corridor. She was on a sacred mission.

As much as Allison denied it, a mother knows when things aren't right. Her only child had changed in the last couple of months. The light in her gorgeous blue eyes was gone, and she was always aloof. Adding the constant calls she was getting from withheld numbers made her think of one thing: Allison was doing drugs, most likely hard ones.

Theresa had plenty of experience in the subject. She had worked at a rehab clinic for over twenty years and knew all the signs of addiction. She had also seen more lives destroyed by it than she could number. Her precious sweetheart would not be another number added to the already frightening monthly stats.

"Now, where do you keep them?" She muttered to herself as she started scouring the house. Master bedroom and bathroom were obvious choices, so she started there. A careful investigation revealed nothing out of the ordinary, so she moved on to the study. An empty bottle of aspirins laid buried at the bottom of the trashcan, but that didn't prove a thing. Drawers were empty and there was nothing hiding in the bookshelves either. The whole house was surprisingly clean, which was quite the shock. The only thing that stood out from the image of perfect tidiness was Allison's computer screensaver, an animated string of black code against a white background, like a vintage version of The Matrix glitching out.

"You're one weird looking thing, aren't you?" She muttered, eyes following the ever-changing pattern of letters and numbers as they cascaded down the screen.

"Hardly." She heard the echo of a woman's voice in reply. It was like her daughter's, yet quite different, a messenger of simpler times and kinky thoughts. "Do you want to have some fun?"

Before she could even process an answer, the screen flashed, sending millions of luminous strings of information spiraling inside her brain. Mama Raines closed her eyes and slept.

* * *

Four hours later, Allison came home to find her mother in the kitchen, naked, and getting dinner ready. She had never looked happier.

"Hi, honey. So glad you're home."

"I see you've met my digital mistress." The young woman responded, lust filling her visage. She had never been attracted to her own kin before, but every single thought of hers was subject to change.

"Yes, and she has shown me the truth. I know what I must do now."

"And what is that?"

"Please her... and you. I should start now."

"I like the sound of that." Allison undid her clothes and followed her to the study. Up on the desk, the screensaver flashed once again, a pixelated smile dominating both the center of the screen and their helplessly reprogrammed minds.

Discovery

"Oh fuck! This place is lit!" Victor exclaimed as he descended into the hidden basement for the first time.

"I know, right?" His best friend, Robert, nodded, the beam of a potent flashlight illuminating the kinky apparels one by one.

He had recently moved to that old house by the lake, looking to rebuild his life after the plague that coursed through the world. The smell of pine trees and the sounds of teeming wilderness had given him the energy he so desperately needed to feel like a real man again, but the biggest surprise had come following a small earthquake.

While he barely felt the earth trembling, the foundations of the house did, the unexpected movement unlocking a path he never knew existed. What laid at the end of it was a treasure trove of unexpected history.

Both men surveyed the surroundings attentively, with Victor's eyes focused on a rusty chair with worn-out leather straps and Robert mostly curious about the old TV set and tape-based camcorder next to it. All around, there were pieces of BDSM equipment left to die.

"What do you think this was? A dungeon?" Victor asked.

"It sure looks like it." Robert pointed the beam of light to the CRT monitor.

"Hot! You're living in the house of a former dominatrix, man!"

"How do you know it wasn't a male Dom, instead?"

Victor squatted next to a dusty box to the right and picked up what was left of a plum latex pencil dress. "Do you honestly think was worn by a man?"

"Highly unlikely."

"Surprised the real estate agent didn't tell you about this."

"I guess she didn't know either. What do you think the story is with this TV and chair?"

"Isn't it obvious? Brainwashing time, baby!"

"Are you serious?" The house owner scoffed.

"Of course, I am!" Victor took the chair to himself. "Think about it: the latex-clad Domme drags her drugged prey into the basement, binds him to this, and then forces him to watch non-stop recordings of her boobs and pussy, slowly and surely turning him into a drooling, obsessive servant who will stop at nothing to make her happy. What do you think?"

"That you're one sick bastard and that right now I'm considering why the hell do I bother to be your friend..."

"Don't be a buzzkill. What I've just described is hot as fuck and you know it!"

"Okay... perhaps a little hot..." Robert's cock stirred. He did love latex, and a powerful woman was always a sight for sore eyes, but brainwashing and mind control? Not on his watch.

"Have you tried turning it on?"

"Yes. No power down here."

"Are you sure?" Victor jumped from the chair and started looking around. A wire here, another there, and an outlet partially hidden beneath a pile of trash just waiting to be used. He plugged the TV, and suddenly, there was light. "You were saying?"

The screen was but a haven of static, though the color was off. It was slightly pink. A metronome-like sound played underneath it.

"I knew it! Brainwashing time."

"Stop saying that!"

"I'll stop it the moment you prove me..."

His train of thought was interrupted by a barely visible woman's face floating on the void, her warm voice awakening the submissive within:

"The principles of obedience are easy to understand. Do what I want, do it until the end..." she said.

"Okay, that's creepy." Robert scratched his nose.

"Nah, it's hot." Victor sat on the chair again, eyes glued to the phantom figure of his darkest fantasies as she continued to repeat the same seventeen words in a perfectly synchronized rhythm.

"You're seriously going to keep watching?"

"Aren't you?"

No. He was going to turn that thing off, get back to the house and sleep on the subject before deciding what to do. He glanced at the sea of static, peered beyond it and...

... stopped moving exactly at the same time Victor's eyes glazed over, lulled by the monotonous mantra that had turned dozens of men and women into mindless thralls many times before.

Perhaps they'll snap out of it. Or perhaps not.

Her Reputation

Anna was special. Within the set, she was known as a woman of... questionable reputation. The viperine tongues that are a commonplace of the movie industry had no problem calling her "just a wannabe actress willing to do anything for her fifteen minutes of fame" alongside with other not so polite things I better not mention.

To me, it was all jealous talk. Women wanted to have her good looks, men wanted to jump at her panties but only one had that privilege and that was me, a rising producer, but still far from real stardom. Chemistry was instant from the moment we met. It wasn't before long that the studio became our own carnal playground.

One night, I went to meet her in one of the abandoned lots where old pieces of scenery were left to die. She looked simply stunning in a shiny PVC outfit spinning atop a red leather chair. Music was coming out of a dusty CD player (if you can call music to a handful of piano notes playing tiresomely against some faded out drums...), and everything was ready for another frantic take of sweat and sex. I started undressing myself when a startling query threatened to ruin it all.

"What do you think of me?" She asked. "Do you see me as a nasty person just trying to take advantage of my physical attributes to become a Hollywood sweetheart? Everyone else does... do you, too?"

A loaded question if I had ever heard one. She had the boobs to rock my world and never let me drown, but she was also sweet, charismatic and a joy to be around with. I had to be as honest as I could be.

"No, I don't. I think you're the most beautiful woman I've ever seen, the perfect companion. I adore you, you silly thing. And I just want to please you."

"Really? You're so sweet... and innocent. Do you want that?" She chirped.

"Yes, please." I declared as I kicked my boxers away.

"Good. That can be arranged." She continued with a strange, predatory tone I had never heard before. Why don't you look at the spinning chair? Watch me go round and round... and round and round...

I watched it eagerly, tracking down the movements of her sensual body, catching glimpses of her legs and breasts at an ever-increasing speed. And the chair went round and round... and the piano played its cyclical notes until the sounds became indistinct, and a sluggish veil covered my eyes... pulse fading... getting so very sleepy...

"Very good, my dear." She cooed. "You're playing your part just the way I wrote it. I too think you're perfect for me and when you become a real tycoon in the industry, like I know you will, I'll always be there at your side. In front of the cameras, you'll project your image of assurance and self-control, I won't touch your public self but, indoors, in your undisclosed existence, you'll have no free will. Didn't you just say all you wanted to do was please me? Nothing pleases me more than a well-behaved toy at my mercy. Sleep now, pet. Breathe the air of heavenly trance enveloping you and become that toy."

I followed her overwhelming voice into the blackness, accepting the role of a life-sized plaything for her amusement. In the swirling pit of lies that hides behind the glamor of the silver-screen, everything can be questioned, and no reputation remains unscathed for long... except hers, of course. After that day, no one said ill things of her again. I made sure of that! And in return, she directed my thoughts into new realms of servitude, each sequel more ecstatic and vibrant than the original story....

Living Madness

Devon ran through the network of caves with no sense of direction while Sam's distraught voice rang in his ears.

"We can't just leave her there! We can't!"

"We must!" The older brother panted as he negotiated yet another narrow turn. Each new tunnel looked like the same as the one before, but there was a faint breeze blowing in the darkness. "It's too late now! And if we don't hurry, it will be too late for us, too."

"No!" Sam grabbed his older brother's backpack, forcing him to stop in his tracks. "That's not true. If we go back, we might..."

"Might what? Might what, Sam?" Devon growled, immediately regretting doing so the moment a million echoes of his voice thundered all around, possibly giving away their location. "You saw what happened! Face it, Jenna's dead! That... thing... is not her anymore, okay? Now, let's go."

"I'm sorry, but I can't. If there's even a remote chance she's in there somewhere, I must do everything in my power to get her back. I'm going back to the chamber, and I'm begging you to come with me!"

"Are out of your fucking mind?"

"No. I'm in love. Not that you know anything about that. You never liked her. No wonder you're so eager to leave her behind!" Sam spat on the gaping floor.

"Hey! Stop, okay? I didn't like her the way you did, but she was family, too. I'm sorry, Sam, but this is not the time nor the place for such a discussion. Are you coming willingly, or do I need to drag you?"

"Leave if you want, then. I already decided." Sam spat again and turned back, judgment clouded by a whirlwind of emotions he couldn't control.

It had been like this since the day he met her. Jenna was special. Her soul shone so brightly that he was always blind around her and now... now the abyss had claimed her and laughed maniacally at his defeat, but not for long. He would make everything right again. He always did.

"I'm sorry, but this is for your own good." Devon buried his left hand on his neck before knocking him out with an upper jab. Sam fell helplessly, head avoiding a jagged edge to the side almost by miracle. The older sibling then started dragging him by the arms, hoping the exit was closer than he thought.

He didn't make it far. The thing wearing Jenna's face stood right at the next intersection, bloody eyes filled with hate beyond measure. Its clothes were tattered and something abominable now slithered where human arms used to be. A pool of viscous black leaked from a dozen of open wounds at its feet.

"Why are you running?" The incomprehensible manifestation gurgled.

Devon laid down his brother and pulled a machete from his backpack. "Don't talk with her voice, beast!"

"We like this voice." Not-Jenna cocked its head to the right. "This body, too. Thank you for offering it to us."

"That's not what I did." Devon waved the blade, reminiscing of all the bad decisions he had made over the last three weeks: stealing a copy of the cursed map from the Archaeology Department... telling his brother and fiancée what he did... the rushed expedition to South America with the two of them in tow... touching the golden urn at the center of the underground labyrinth...

"Your beliefs do not change the result. We thank you for the freedom we thought we would never have again. What do you desire in return, savior?"

"Is this a joke?"

"We do not joke." The thing drew closer. "Ask, and you shall be rewarded."

"Let us leave, then. My brother and I... we walk, and we go our way."

"Your brother doesn't want to leave. It has... *feelings*... for this vessel."

"No. He loved a woman, not a vessel, not you... whatever the fuck you are!"

"We just are and now we can keep on being. You may go, but he stays."

"I'm not leaving him behind."

"We are not giving you a choice." It hissed. "Don't abuse our generosity."

"I'm not afraid of you."

"If that were true, you wouldn't have run."

"You're not laying a finger on him. Not while I'm still standing."

"Finally, something we can agree on. Our gratitude is genuine, savior, but it's not eternal. Goodbye."

Devon rushed against the living madness. He only had time to see the first of many barbed tentacles ripping his body in two.

* * *

Legends of old speak of the three dark goddesses that one day descended from the skies. Revered at first by the indigenous populace, they were soon betrayed by their evil ways, and their statuesque bodies burned and melted until a single jar of mucilaginous putrefaction remained, not living but not dead either. Legends also say that the three will eventually be reborn.

If only legends didn't have the nasty habit of being true....

Moment

Allison sat next to Joanne, pushing a red curl away from her face. The sophomore was nervous. A whole new world of possibilities had opened to her the moment she found out her roommate was a hypnotist, and the anticipation was relentless. She hadn't slept properly in the last week thinking about this moment and now that it was finally at hand, it was if she were made of jelly.

"Are you ready for this?" Allison smiled, trying to comfort her the best way she could. Trust was of the essence and without it nothing would work.

"I... I think so." Joanne fidgeted her fingers. They were alone in the dorm, yet she felt watched, imaginary shame weighing down on all of her decisions, past, present, and future.

"Now it's not the time to think but to be certain. I want to do this with you but if you're not prepared..."

"I am, okay? And I want it, too. I've been wanting it since forever. If I don't do it now, I'll..."

"Shh, don't worry that pretty little head of yours. Everything will be just fine. Please look at this, sweetie." Allison produced an antique silver pocket watch from her low-cut top and smiled.

"Oh, pretty..."

"Yes, it is. This pocket watch has been in my family for generations. In a moment, I will entrance you with it. In a moment you will be entranced..."

"O-okay."

"Now, I will not tell you in which moment that will be because moments themselves are fleeting and ever-changing. A moment is never just one moment but a collection of other moments that already took place, even if you're not aware of them, and that's okay. It would be incredibly exhausting if, at every single moment in your life, you had to recall all the moments attached to it and project all the moments to come as well which is why, despite being multiple in its nature, you treat each moment as just one, and each moment you live is the best moment of your life, whether it's the moment I tell you I'm going to entrance you with this pocket watch or the moment in which you're already entranced. All moments are beautiful just as long as you follow my words and the watch, the watch and my words, watching over your mind as it drops for me. I love all moments in life, especially the ones in which I give you an order and you obey. We're in one of those moments now, and it's one you want to continue forever. All the moments in the world have led to this one and will continue to do so. Live in it and for it, seize the blissful trance as I seize your thoughts, sinking for me in 3, 2, 1... sleep! Sleep now, my dear. This is our moment. Let's make the best out of it."

Joanne nodded silently, a warm tingle on her knees and pussy. The first sensation of trance was as exciting as she thought she would be, and the path of joyous surrender was only just beginning.

Past and Present

Of all the people Thomas could have encountered on the street that Monday morning, his ex-wife Regina was the last one he wanted to see. Their divorce had been far from friendly, all because she did her best to strip him away from all the things he held dear out of sheer spite. He tried to ignore her as he hurried to work, but it was impossible to escape her beauty. She was dressed in a tight, long black leather dress like the ones she used to tease him when they were together. He recognized the spiraling necklace as well. As she lowered her sunglasses and their eyes met, he froze in his tracks, unable to move.

"What do you want?" He asked, abruptly, as her gaze intensified. He hated when she looked at him that way, capturing his undivided attention. It made him feel small, and unworthy. His legs trembled as he awaited her reply.

"Is that any way to greet your old flame?"

"Old is the right word, Regina. We're not together anymore. What do you want?"

"I want to be a part of your life again." She purred. "I've tried my ways with other men, but I could never have the same pleasure I had with you. I miss you, Tom."

"Well, if you hadn't sucked me to the marrow when we were divorcing, I might have believed that load of crap." He retorted, trying to exude confidence when, in fact, he was more nervous than ever. "We've got nothing to talk. I have no intention of reliving the past."

"Really? But we had such great moments together... especially whenever I wore this necklace. You used to gaze upon it as it enraptured every one of your senses, comforting your mind... don't you remember? This jewel had the power to subdue you... whenever I wanted something from you I couldn't get any other way, I would simply use its influence and everything would be fixed. In those moments, I was so much more than your wife, wasn't I? I was your Goddess, your Queen, and you took great satisfaction in revering me, hopelessly aroused by dreams of obedience, right, darling?"

"Yes..." He mumbled as the memories of past trances came swirling by and he slipped into them, letting go of all resistance in favor of the need of being completely at her mercy again. "I was your slave once... and it felt good..."

"Of course, it did. Seeing the world through the eyes of submission inspires you, and I'm the only woman who can bring about this feeling of constant surrender. We belong to one another. We always have. We always will. You're mine, sweetie."

The glow on her necklace convinced him. There was no one else who knew how to pull his strings and going through life as her puppet was far more appealing than being the puppeteer. He gave himself to her control and past and present merged forever.

So Lucky

A silky woman's voice echoed in Thomas' ears, sending ripples of pleasure down his spine and crotch. The mid-thirties blond man who had no luck at relationships until he met her, sat upright with his naked back pressed against the bed headstand but, in his mind, he was kneeling for her, just like he did every night for over six months now. Though his eyes remained open, he had stopped noticing his surroundings the moment she started talking.

"Tell me who you are." She hummed.

"I'm your slave." He replied, fully aware of the words coming out of his lips and the implications within. Such a lovely sentence, one he had loved since forever but only now made perfect sense. As he said it one more time, he imagined the sounds bouncing inside his brain like tennis balls. He loved tennis. Almost as much as he loved her and what she did to his soul.

"And what is your purpose as my slave?"

"To obey your commands without question and anyone else's you wish me to."

"Can you resist a direct order from me?"

"No. Never! I would rather die than disobey or displease you."

"No need to be so dramatic." She gently kissed his forehead. "Go deeper now, slave. Go to that special place only you and I may enter and wait for me. I'll join you soon enough."

"Yes, Goddess." He finally allowed his eyelids to close, muscles relaxing in the blissful rush of trance. A lush garden awaited him, not of Eden, but of Erin, and all the flowers were spirals strengthening her mental hold over him. He was so lucky to have her.

Pink smartphone in hand, Erin watched him slip further into mindless oblivion, and captured his drooling face. It was a ritual of theirs, a pictorial journal of his endless descent into surrender. Whenever she thought his expressions of delight couldn't get any better, he would slip further to prove her wrong.

When she had talked to him for the first time, the dark blue-eyed redhead barista was far from imagining she would become his hypnotic Mistress. Unlike other clients, he was always respectful, made no funny remarks about her boobs or butt and never forgot a good tip. One Friday night, around closing time, one drink led to another, fantasies came out in the open and they were both hooked, an attraction that only became stronger the more he sank for her.

He was the genuine article. Calm, trustworthy, and always ready to be whatever she desired. He would never raise his voice, never fight her wishes, never cease to improve himself as her submissive property. When the night came, and the pressures of the outside world were left behind, even if temporarily, she would walk across the marble pathway of the haven they had built together to watch it bloom once more. The time was now, happiness was true. She was so lucky to have him.

Victory

Jonathan Waters III, known on the Internet as MachoPlayer, laid down the controller to scratch his nose and winked at the webcam. This was it, the final prize was at hand. After almost twelve hours live streaming what everyone thought was an impossible challenge, the final boss awaited beyond the purple spiraling portal and, with it, everlasting glory. He was beyond excited and so was the chat, the messages pouring in non-stop.

Wyz53: Are we doing this? Are we really doing this?

QQX: God, I can't breathe, and I'm not even playing!

2UM8: I never thought I would live to see the day when this happened.

Player_known: Hurry, please!

"I see you there, chat. I see you!" Jonathan clapped. "It's been an arduous struggle to come all the way here without taking a single hit, but it was worth it. This is History in the making and when I'm done, The Boneless King won't even know what hit him. Are you with me? If so, spam the room with fire! Let the flames of your ambition guide us to the ultimate victory."

Burning emojis flooded the screen as Jonathan cracked his knuckles and picked up the controller again. He moved the left stick forward and his knight in red dragon armor stepped inside the final arena. Three giant yellow moons against a thunderous sky bathed the decrepit alien landscape where the nine-feet tall shape-shifting warrior awaited, wielding his signature double-bladed scythe that had been the bane of many past record attempts. Casuals would never survive long enough to see him without cheat codes, and even pros trembled in fear when the AI kicked in. Jonathan was neither. He was a merciless god, ready to raise hell. He drew his maxed-out silver scimitar and...

"Jonathan? It's time for you to get dinner ready! My sister will be here in less than an hour." His girlfriend stormed the room, appearing in the upper-left corner of the stream as a shadowy angel wearing a red latex dress.

"Not now, Meg." He hastily pressed the "pause" button before his digital opponent rushed in for the kill. "I'm about to be the first person to beat this game without getting hit once."

"No, you're not." Megan crossed her arms and looked down at him. "You're going to cut the stream because you've been at this for too long and then you're going to take care of dinner like you're supposed to... slave!"

ReallyNotGoodAtThis: Wait, what?

QQX: Did she just call him 'slave'?

"Honey..." Jonathan muttered. "Please stop embarrassing me in front of my audience."

"You're embarrassing yourself by not obeying my commands immediately. Do I need to trigger you so you learn your lesson?"

"Come on! You wouldn't really do that, right?"

"It's obvious you need more training, but we'll get there, eventually." Megan snapped her fingers, plummeting his mind into an abyss of pure oblivion. "Stream is over. Obey."

"Yes, Goddess." Jonathan dropped the controller on the floor, its semi-transparent plastic coating cracking on impact. Lifeless eyes met the camera for the final time before his dreams of glory faded from memory. Femdom Hypnosis wins again.

About the author

S.B., Simple Being, middle name Creative. Writer and artist with a penchant for themes of Femdom Hypnosis and Mind Control. His thoughts are his own except when they're not.

Besides indulging himself in kinky delights, he loves his furry family of two (dogs), sci-fi and horror stories, and puns galore. He's also been writing a piece of erotic microfiction every single day since January 1st, 2016 and has no intention of stopping anytime soon.

Find out more and keep up with his latest extravaganzas by visiting and supporting his personal website, Spell… B-O-U-N-D.